A LOVE FROZEN IN BLOOD

DAKSHINA VIJAYAKUMAR

To,

my Amma and Achan who supported me in my every decision and gave me the strength to pursue my dreams.

Contents

Acknowledgements

I have to start by thanking my parents who have always supported my dreams and my pillars of strength. Next I would like to thank my friend Amaze, who supported me greatly in writing this book. From reading through each chapters to giving honest feedbacks, she helped a lot in structuring and completing this book. Next I would like to thanks my friends Gowri, Pooja and Amalu for being my constant source of support and encouragement. I would also like to thanks my sister and biggest cheerleader Parvathy for boosting my morale throughout the process of writing this book. Lastly, I would like to thank God Almighty for giving me the strength to push through all the tough times and helping me to complete this book.

Prologue

Hannah was always a curious kid growing up. As a kid, she liked thrillers more than cartoons. Her parents brushed off this curiosity as a harmless interest, but her best fiend knew that she was constantly getting into trouble because of this curiosity. Each new case she found in the newspapers or online articles got her excited and she spent days trying to draw her own conclusion. Sometimes, she went as far as to visit the various crime scenes to read more into case. It was only last month that Hannah was warned by the local police detective to stop poking her head into where it did not belong. But that didn't stop her from jumping to the next exciting story she found. But, will this new story pull her into depths which she didn't desire to go into?

CHAPTER ONE

"Hannah! It's time for college!"

"I don't want to go today! Please let me sleep mama!"

"You skipped your class yesterday! You are definitely going today! No excuses!! Get up now or I will throw you out of the bed in 5"

Being fed up with mom's nagging, I got up and rubbed my eyes.

"Shoot! It's only Tuesday", I cursed mentally before getting ready for college. I grabbed a toast from the dining table and ran for the door.

"Bye Mama!", I shouted, sprinting out of the house.

"Hey Cece! Are you coming today?", I texted Cece walking down the road. Cece or otherwise known as Celia is my best friend. We met during high school and somehow, she has still managed to stick by me even after witnessing my eccentricities.

"Yup! On my way."

I walked faster upon receiving her text to catch the bus to my college. I am studying at Westwood University, a quiet and calm university in the countryside of England. I study Psychology and this is my second year of college. After a rough bus ride for about 2 hours, I finally reached college.

"Cece!", I screamed as I saw her by the lockers.

"I thought you were going to ditch me today too."

"I didn't mean to skip yesterday. I just had a really bad stomach ache, you know." "Oh! Give it a rest Hannah! I am not Prof. Briggs to buy your stomach ache story. I very well know you skipped it because it rained."

"Well! You know me too well!"

"One more time you do this, I am severing all ties with you. Stupid!"

"Nope! Not again"

We walked to our class. The first hour was Developmental psychology and Prof.Warren was going on and on about the theories and concepts. My nose almost touched the desk when Cece hit me on my shoulder.

"What?!"

"Did you hear about that boy in Engineering major?"

"Which boy? Is he cute?", I asked with a smirk.

"Idiot! The boy who jumped down the bridge!"

"What the?! Who is that and why did he jump off a freaking bridge?!!"

"The police haven't said why but it almost looks like bullying gone wrong." "We are in college for god's sake! Who the hell does that in college?"

"Don't know it is just a speculation. The real reason might be something else." Before I could ask anything else, we were interrupted by the shrill shriek of Prof.Warren asking us to shut up. Throughout the lecture the thought lingered in my brain. A dead boy from my university who suddenly jumped off a bridge.

"Strange", I thought as the bell rang to release us from the boring depths of developmental psychology. Walking back to the locker, my mind was still with the boy. "Cece, what was his name?"

"Whose?"

"The guy who jumped off the bridge"

"Joy"

"Cool", I muttered absent mindedly as I stuffed my books back in the locker. "Hannah, if this is going to be your next investigation project, I am going to whack your head! Last time you got caught up in something like this it lasted for months!"

"Don't worry Cece baby, I have it under control", I replied with a wink.

Cece already knew I was going to be too involved with Joy and his story.

CHAPTER TWO

"Hannah! Do you want me to drop you at the bus stop?"

"No. I am staying back for a meeting with the social service club."

"Cool! Bye then."

"Adios"

I walked to the small building near the basketball court. That is where the social service club meets.

"Hi Hannah! I am glad you stayed back for the meeting."

I was greeted by the wide grin of Jaine, our club secretary. I rarely stay back for the meetings, hence the over enthusiasm. Throwing my backpack on the nearby couch, I noticed a poster on the brick wall behind Janie.

"JUSTICE FOR JOY "

And above the bold heading was the picture of a boy who had the most beautiful eyes I had ever seen. His eyes were the color of freshly polished silver. Even though the picture seemed old, his eyes were sparkling. Just above his crescent shaped eyelids, his hazelnut hair fell lazily. There were careless curls resting peacefully over his head and a small yet welcoming smile was plastered on his face. I was mesmerized. I was captivated. No one! I repeat, no one has caused this effect on me. I stood there caught in a trance, falling deeper and deeper into his crystal orbs. I was shaken back into reality by Anvar who shoved a can of coke into my hands. "Wake up dumbhead! Stop staring at a dead person."

It was then I realized I was staring at a dead person. He seemed so alive until a few seconds ago. Without realizing, I slowly muttered under my breath,

"Why did you have to die?"

I was brought back once again by the shrill shriek of Janie who was struggling to get everybody's attention.

"Okay guys. We have gathered here to discuss something really important. As we all know, our dear companion has left us, leaving us in distress and doubts. The college, police and the mainstream media are refusing to speak the truth.

They have decided to side line the story of our Joy and are supporting his perpetrators. We shall not abide by this silence. He was one of us and we shall seek justice for him!"

"One of us?!" I asked myself.

"Excuse me Janie!", I said.

"What exactly happened to Joy? I have never seen him around."

"If you came to meetings regularly, you might have seen him.", Dean replied with a hint of sarcasm.

"What?!"

"Hannah, Joy had been a regular in our meetings. You might have seen him.", Janie said.

"Oh! Okay"

"How could I miss this guy?! I should have come here more often. Shit!", I mentally cursed myself.

"And coming back to your question," continued Janie, "Joy was found dead under the Rockwood Bridge near the park on Saturday morning by two elderly who had gone there for an early morning walk. It was ruled out a suicide after autopsy but there was no suicide note to be found. The police are assuming that he took his life due to love failure but his friends and family are sure that he never had any girlfriend. There were no known incidents of bullying. He was quite the model student in school and college. He was a very warm and welcoming person." I found my eyes getting wet unknowingly. I dabbed my eyes on my sleeves and listened carefully.

"We have started this movement to get Joy the justice he deserves. His family has promised to support the cause and help us in any way possible."

There was pin drop silence in the room as Janie finished speaking.

"So, Janie, what is your plan?" Anwar broke the silence.

"We are planning to gather evidence from his friends and well as family and try to find the reason he decided to take his life. Today we are going to his house to visit his mother and also go through his room so we can understand him better."

"But isn't that a crime scene?"

"No. Since he did not die in his room it is not. Is there anyone who isn't willing to come today?" "I am scared. I am not coming." Rhea said, looking as white as snow.

"Okay. Are the rest of you in?"

"Yes!"

"Okay let's get moving!"

My gut was telling me that this visit is going to change a lot of things for me. It was the first time I was feeling strange after hearing the news of someone's death. I was feeling something else, a sense of closeness and affection and longing for someone I have never met. Someone who was lying deep inside the earth.

CHAPTER THREE

The bike ride to Joy's house wasn't pleasant as I had to clutch on to the sweaty t-shirt of Anvar. Once I arrived there, it was nothing like I imagined. A well-built house which gave a warm feeling just as I looked at it. The walls were covered with ivy climbers on one side and an old man sat on the porch reading the newspaper.

"Grandpa, it's us!" Jaine certainly looks like she has been here more than once.

"Oh! Darling! I thought you forgot about us. I did not see you after the funeral." "Oh! It is not like that grandpa; I have been a little busy at college. Look, all of Joy's friends are here. We will go meet his mom now."

"Yes yes. Go on. She will be happy seeing you."

As we moved inside, a cozy living room welcomed us. The room was neat and well kept. There was not even a pillow that was out of place. I was surprised to find everything so well kept. In the corner of the room, another picture of Joy was kept up on a small table.

"Those eyes! I can't seem to get over it!"

The more I looked, the more I seemed to get lost in them. They were inviting, there was a certain charm to it that drew me closer and closer.

"Oh! Hi kids. I am happy that you people came by." Joy's mom said with a small smile. Contrary to the warm and cozy house, his mother was a mess. There were dark circles under her eyes and she looked really fragile. She was nothing like her charming son. Or maybe, the loss of her son had turned her into this fragile mess.

"Hi aunty. How are you?"

"What can I say? I feel like there is nothing left anymore."

"Please don't say like that aunty." interrupted Dean. "If you give up, Jia will be more devastated!"

"Jia?! Did he have a sister?!"

"Hey! Hey Anvar!" I slowly called to Anvar who was standing beside me. "Did Joy have a sister?"

"You really don't know anything right?!"

I smiled in embarrassment.

"Joy had two sisters. But last year their family met with an accident and Joy's dad and elder sister passed away. He was at a college event that time. Only his mother and younger sister survived."

"Oh!"

While Jaine was consoling the mother who was devastated, my eyes roamed around the house. There were not many pictures on the walls. It looks like they went for minimalism. The decor was simple too.

"Aunty, shall we go to Joy's room to have a look around?"

"Sure kids! Please find those who drove Joy to this. He would not do this on his own. He will never leave me alone!" and aunty broke into tears. Jaine hugged her tightly and calmed her down after which we went to Joy's room.

There were three rooms on the second floor. I think it was for the three siblings. I thought about the youngest one. She would have to wake up every day to two empty rooms. It might be really hard on her to lose two siblings within a span of a year. Joy's room was neat. Very neat. The shelves were well arranged. The walls were filled with posters of random pictures.

"He looks like he is a photographer"

"Can you stop drooling?"

"Can you stop annoying me?" I glared at Anvar.

Jaine spent a good 20 minutes going through every drawer and cupboard. I started feeling uneasy so I came out of the room. As I came out, I saw one of the two closed doors open slightly. A tiny head peeped out of the slightly open door.

I smiled at the tiny figure looking at me. "Hai! You must be Jia! How are you?"

She did not reply but extended her tiny hands out of the door.

"Do you want me to come in?"

She nodded. I was scared but decided to go in with her.

"What is it Jia?"

"I know you."

"Me? How? It is the first time I am seeing you. You must be mistaken"

"No. It is not my first time seeing you. I have seen you, in Joy's pictures."

"Pictures?"

The tiny figure retreated to the cupboard near her bed. This room was the exact opposite of Joy's.

There was an eerie feeling to it. A cold shiver ran through the spine. She came back with a small brown envelope.

"Here."

I opened the envelope and a set of 5 or 6 pictures were inside and all of them were me. The pictures were taken when I was not looking. But they were beautiful. I had never seen myself looking so pretty. I was surprised. Shocked. There was a train of emotions going through me.

But before I could process all that, I had a lot of questions. Before I could ask anything, Jia said, "Joy loved you."

I stood there frozen unable to process what I just heard.

CHAPTER FOUR

I couldn't process anything. Everything around me came to a standstill. Suddenly I heard someone pushing the door open. I was startled but quickly stuffed the envelope back into my bag. "Hey! What are you doing here?"

Before I could answer Jia replied to Dean.

"I just called her in because she reminded me of my sister."

Dean mouthed an "oh!" and left quietly.

"Jia, I need to go. I will call you later."

"Okay. You need to help Joy. You need to find the truth about him."

Without thinking the reply came out of my mouth, "I will!"

I don't know why I said that to the kid. But going back home, neither the bumpy road nor the sweaty t-shirt of Anvar bothered me. I was too lost in Joy.

Reaching home, I did not spare a glance at my mother who was in the kitchen and ran to my room. I could hear mom's worried voice asking me if I was alright. I told her I will talk to her after sometime.

One thing about my family is that they have always given me my space. They have always respected my privacy and my decisions. So, it was easy to be myself even around my parents. I threw myself onto my bed and watched the fan go round and round. Everything that happened today was too much to take in for me. I looked at the ceiling and wondered, if I had met Joy before, he would have still been around. I could have saved him. Without realizing, I was sobbing hard into the pillows. Suddenly I felt like I lost a part of me.

But I questioned myself, "How can this happen?! I just found out about him today. How can he become so important?" This is not my casual obsession with death and its reasons. This is something more. Something that is going to flip my world upside down. I looked at the photos again and again and realized how much love was there in those pictures.

I pictured myself fighting and teasing Joy because I looked ugly in a picture. I could hear him saying that I always looked beautiful. I could feel his heart beating on my cheeks as I hugged him. If only he was alive.

I was brought back to my senses when I saw Cece's message flash on my phone screen.

"Hannah! I saw in the class group that you people visited Joy's house. How was it?" I couldn't tell Cece everything now, at least not through text. She might not believe me. So, I decided to play it cool.

"You mean how the house looked? It was average." I texted back.

"You idiot. You know what I asked about."

"Everyone was sad. It looked like Joy was really the joy of his house. Are you free tonight?"

"Yeah. why?"

"Come over."

"Okay"

I kept the pictures in the drawer next to my bed and took out my laptop. I searched for Joy's name and started reading the news.

"A college student was found dead. Police thinks its suicide"

"The boy who took his life-the toxic college culture"

"Once again a poor soul leaves for heaven due to broken heart"

The headings varied. Some even claimed devil worship. I got annoyed at how people take advantage of a death to sell their news. While I was scrolling up and down a certain headline caught my attention.

"Death of College boy-possibility of murder"

It was intriguing to find something other than college bullying and broken heart. I read through the news.

"The 20-year-old boy whose body was found by the bridge is raising too many questions. The police and mainstream media had side lined this case calling it a mere suicide. But that is not the case. This 20-year-old Engineering major was an active participant in an online chatroom titled, 'The troubled teens'. As a result of the special investigation of our team, we came to know that this is a group that speaks about the corruption and issues in the society and find ways to tackle them. There is a high chance that one such endeavor led to the boy's body being found under the bridge. Unfortunately, after the boy's death the chatroom was deleted. Our investigation team is trying to get more details. Stay tuned for more."

I wondered why this never came up. The article did not have many views either. So, I decided to check out the page.

"The Legendary Herald"

"Wow! Nice name."

After going through several of their posts, I understood why there were less views under the article. This news website had a history of exaggerating news. But a part of me felt that Joy's news was not an exaggeration. There might be some truth to it. Hence, I decided that I will contact the editor and get more details.

"Chief Editor: Mr. Samuel Lian John

email: yoursammy1965@gmail.com"

"Oh! He is a boomer." I made a remark while noting down the mail id.

I sat down to mail the editor for more details. I was determined. I knew I had to find the truth. I knew I had to do this for Joy because,

"I love him"

I think I said that aloud because the next thing I hear is Cece screaming from my door.

"You love whom?"

CHAPTER FIVE

"You love who?"

"Shut up! Mom will hear and I don't love anyone!"

"I just heard!!"

"Maybe you are drunk?"

I was trying my best to make it all a hallucination and clearly, I was doing a bad job.

"I am what?"

"Drunk!"

"Shut up stupid! I know what I heard."

"Oh! I was talking about Robert Pattinson."

"You don't like him", she said looking annoyed. Yes, I am not a big fan of Robert Pattinson. Twilight did it.

"But I love him now!"

"Okay. I am not going to ask again. Tell me when you feel like it."

Okay, so this is Cece's last weapon. When she says this, I always end up spilling everything. Like always, it happened this time too.

"Okay. But promise me you won't get mad."

"When have I ever got mad?"

I mentally counted all the instances when she almost ripped my head apart. I opened my drawer and showed her the envelope.

"What's in this?"

"Open and see"

"Oh, my GOD!!!!!! You look so pretty! Are you in love with the guy who took the pictures? I am not blaming you then. Okay! Tell me! When are we meeting him!"

My eyes became moist. If only Joy was alive, I would have jumped around and screamed to my best friend about how this guy was so in love with me and how I am so happy to have him. I looked down and smiled before telling her the truth.

"Joy. He is the one who took the pictures"

"Joy? Wait! I remember the name. What! What?!!" her eyes were almost out of her head.

"Yes. It is the same Joy."

"Are you mad? Are you out of your freaking mind?! Are you insane to fall in love with a dead person?"

I remember asking the same questions to myself an hour or two before. I still don't have answers. I simply looked down and waited for her to stop screaming. After she cooled down, I narrated the entire story. When I finished, Cece was crying. She pulled me into a hug and said, "I am sorry Hannah. I am really sorry. I understand how you feel."

This was the best part about Cece she always understands. Even if she burns the whole house down, she understands.

"But you do know that this is pure madness. You cannot love someone who is dead." "I know. But I can't help this. I could have prevented all this if I just noticed him before."

"Hannah! Stop blaming yourself. What he did was his decision. How could you have known what is going on in his head when you haven't even had a talk with him?"

"I don't know Cece. The only thing I am sure of is that I want answers. I want answers as to why he did this. Not just for me, but for his family and everyone else who loved him. I have to do this."

"Hannah! You are going to lose yourself in this blind chase. You do understand this is going to take a toll on you. I can't stand aside and let you fall through."

"Cece, I understand. I understand that I might lose my sanity over this. But I have to do this. I am not backing down from this."

"Argh! Fine. But you are not doing this alone."

"Cece! I can't drag you into this."

"You are not dragging me, I am coming with you"

I did not argue anymore. Maybe it was my selfishness, but I knew I needed Cece with me in this fight.

"Okay. Tell me what you were doing?"

I explained to her about the strange article.

"Fine. Let's send an email to that guy."

I sat down to type.

"Sir,

I came across your article about the death of a college student. I am his friend and would like to know more on why you thought his death was a murder. I want to let people know the truth about his death. I kindly request you to reply as soon as possible.

Thanks,

Hannah J Hopkin"

I pressed the send button. I had officially launched myself into this. Things were getting real. Cece noticed me zoning out. She asked me to get ready and took me out for a late-night snack. There is a 24-hour supermarket right around the corner. After ice cream, I felt very composed. Cece took a cab back home and I was walking back. Reaching home, I was so tired that I would fall asleep if I just closed my eyes. I changed into my nightwear and got ready to sleep. Suddenly my phone screen lightened up with a notification.

"Gmail: You have a new mail from Samuel Lian John"

I jumped up and opened the mail.

"Will share more details in person. Come to Ricco's restaurant at 6PM tomorrow. I will be wearing a blue jacket and a baseball hat"

My jaw dropped. A hundred questions ran through my brain about meeting this guy in person. Will it be safe? What if he kidnaps me? What if he kills me?

Again, my reckless gut feeling was telling me to go for it. And since I had nothing else to work on, I decided to follow this lead. I put my thoughts aside and texted Cece.

"We need to go somewhere tomorrow"

Cece replied almost immediately.

"Where?"

"To Ricco's"

"That place is shady."

"I know. That editor guy is meeting us there"

"You really are going to get us killed"

"Trust me in this"

"I am trusting you. Let's get this done"

"Cool. See you"

"Bye"

The hunt has officially begun. Now, there is no turning back.

CHAPTER SIX

Ricco's was shady. Shady. Really shady.

Going in, we were welcomed by the strong smell of cigarettes and alcohol. No one was sober there. From the servers to the customers, everyone was drunk.

"Hannah, are you sure this is the place?"

"Yes"

"I don't think we will make it alive out of here"

"Cece! Don't be scared!"

Even though I told Cece to not be scared, I was shaking from head to toe. As we advanced further into the badly lit cafe, all the eyes, red, with not even an ounce of sanity stared right at us. We stood rooted to where we were standing.

"Tom! Look at these young treats! Did you get them for us?"

"Shut up! I can't afford young girls"

"Maybe they are in need of some money. Come here baby girl. Come. On my lap. I will show you some good stuffs"

Cece tugged on my sleeves signaling me to run out. As we took a step back, one of the men who were sitting started to come towards us.

"Where do you think you are going baby girl? We didn't even start!"

He showed his teeth which were covered in brown residue from years of smoking. We were even scared to move. Just when he was within an arm's distance, a hoarse voice echoed from the far end of the cafe.

"They are with me. Leave them alone."

The voice seemed to scare everyone around. The eyes fixed on us were withdrawn and the brown toothed man retreated back to his seat. There he is! The baseball hat. That must be Samuel. We ran towards him.

"Why the hell would you ask us to meet here of all the places?"

"Calm down. I know this must have scared you but I have my reasons. Sit down"

We sat down fuming with anger. He looked calm. So calm that it was ticking us off.

"Tell me. What did you mean in that article of yours?"

"Wow. Straight to business. I like it."

"Please. We don't want to spend time here. Please answer our questions."

"Okay."

He took out a crimson-colored diary from his bag and pushed it across the table. Before I could ask, he started to talk.

"On the day Joy died, I wanted to report his family's response first. So, on hearing the news I rushed to his house, only to find his little sister there. All the others had gone to verify his body. The kid looked smart. I asked her to take me to Joy's room and I went through his room trying to find anything that would be a hot headline. Shuffling through the wardrobe I found this diary hidden safely among his clothes. I took it home to read and found out about the chatroom and the issues related to it. Joy had been warned by a business group, when he tried to uncover their shady deal. But he did not stop there."

Samuel opened a page in the diary.

"See this entry. Read it"

"21st June 2021

Today, I followed them to the building site. The man in the red suit was talking to a few people who looked like officials. They were listening keenly to the red suit man. I managed to take some photos. I was spotted by the red man's bodyguard. I escaped narrowly. Now that they have seen my face, my life might be in danger. The officials looked like government people. I should be careful."

"Why did you not show this to the police?"

"You see the sentence mentioned here, the officials looked like government people. I did not want to jeopardize the only chance to find the truth about Joy's death"

"Oh! But how are we going to find this red man?"

"See, that is the problem. Joy has not mentioned the red man's identity or the organization he worked for in this entire diary. I swept through it three times. Not even a word. Joy has mentioned some photographs. They were neither in his room nor his laptop"

"How do you know?"

"Remember, I swept through his room. I had a look at his laptop that day. The little kid knew the password."

"Did you ask the kid about this man?"

"Joy knew this man was dangerous. I don't think he will put his sister in danger by passing on that information"

"So how are we going to find him?"

"Coming to that. I went through his room and also the list of articles that were discovered along with his body. There was no information about his phone and camera. His family assumed some passerby stole it"

"That can be the case"

"I don't think so. He had a watch on him which was as expensive as his phone. If robbery had been the intent, that would have been stolen. His wallet was also intact on his body."

"Do you mean?"

"Yes. The people who killed him took it."

"How are we going to find them?"

"For that we need to know who the man in the red suit is."

"And how are we supposed to do that?"

"Go through anyone he might have been in contact with. If we had the list of participants in that chatroom, we could have worked on that. But that chatroom disappeared into thin air. Let me see if I can work on that. By that time, you guys ask around the college."

"Sure"

"Okay bye. You can keep the diary. Here is my visiting card. Call me if anything comes up"

"Okay. But how did you know you can trust me?"

"Go to the diary entry of August 11th"

"11th August 2021

It was her birthday today. I clicked a few pictures from a distance. I wanted to run to her and wish her Happy Birthday. I want to take her out on a nice date. Hah! Maybe next year. There are a lot of things I have to deal with and I don't want her to be caught in the crossfire. I love her so much. Her smile is THE BEST!

I love you, Hannah. Happy Birthday to you"

Below the entry, there was a polaroid picture of me laughing. Involuntarily, tears ran down my cheek.

"This is how I know I can trust you. I did not rescue you immediately when you came into the cafe because I had to crosscheck. Sorry about that. And I picked this place because, ever since I published that article, they have their eyes on me. I saw people lurking around my office and house. I did not want to put you guys in danger. Call me if something is up. Bye"

I sat there with tears slowly wetting the end of his diary.

"Hannah! Come on we have to get out of here"

Cece somehow pulled me out of the cafe and caught a cab somewhere down the road. I was mechanically following her instructions. We reached home and Cece woke me up from my trance.

"Hannah! We are home"

"I will find the person who took Joy from me. I will not forgive him"

"Hannah, what are you...?"

"Yes. This is not just for Joy. This is for me. I did not notice him when he was around me. The least I could do is give a purpose to his death. I cannot let people think he died without a reason." Cece just stared at me. She knew I wouldn't back down. So, she did what she could. Held my hands and decided to walk with me through this.

CHAPTER SEVEN

I couldn't sleep. All night I sat up and read his diary. He had mentioned me a lot of times. Each time my name popped up, I cried.

"Why? Why did it have to be this way!"

The only thing I could do now was get justice for him and I was determined I would do that.

Next morning, I woke up with puffed up eyes and a bad headache. My mom knew something was up, but didn't ask.

"You should take care of yourself"

"I know mom. It is just a tough time at college"

Cece was waiting for me in front of the class. She looked equally distressed. We didn't talk much until the lecture began.

"Hannah, you found something?"

"None."

"Anything in his dairy?"

"I was pretty much crying throughout it. I couldn't focus on details"

"Hannah! You promised me you won't lose yourself"

"I won't"

"But-"

"Who is talking while I am teaching?! Do you think you are better than me? Why don't you come up here and teach!"

My head was already on the verge of splitting apart and I couldn't take this lame old camel shouting! I took my books and walked out of the class.

"HANNAH!! WHAT DO YOU THINK YOU ARE DOING? GET BACK. NOW!!!" The old camel was still shouting and Cece was trying her best in apologizing. I just pretended not to hear and walked towards the basketball court. Cece came behind panting.

"What the hell did you do right now?"

"My head was hurting and he was getting on my nerves."

"You really are aiming for suspension. Aren't you?"

"Maybe"

"This girl!!"

I sat on one of the seats in the gallery and took out the crimson diary. I started to read through it again.

"Are you going to read it again?"

"Yes. I need to see if there is anything in it."

While I was reading, Cece was going through her phone.

"Ouch"

"What?", I asked as Cece was bent over looking at her feet.

"Something bit me"

"Might be an ant", I said and resumed reading the diary.

Cece was letting out loud moans looking at her feet.

"Cece, get a grip. It's just an ant bite"

"What if it is a poisonous ant!", she said looking up.

"Are you listening to yourself?", I asked, laughing off her strange worry.

"Wait Hannah, look!"

"I don't have time to check your ant bite"

"No! It's not that! Look at this!", she said pointing at the back cover of the diary.

"What?"

"It is glued together"

"What? What are you saying?"

"Are you deaf? See this cover of the diary! It is glued together. See the edges, it looks like someone cut it open"

"Shit! Why didn't I notice it before?"

"Should have probably stopped crying"

"Shut up! Let me tear this first"

I slowly tried to separate the glued parts. It was glued pretty tight. After a few tries, I ripped it open.

"No: 198

password: 1108"

"The password! It's your birthday!"

"Shut up Cece! That is not important! What is this password and number? It is too short to be the username of any profile."

On the left-hand page, there was something else written.

"Hannah, look here!"

"Left to the fountain.

3rd to the right"

"This looks like an address."

"How are we supposed to find this? There are hundreds of fountains in this country"

"Samuel! Cece, call him!"

"The reporter guy?"

"Yeah! Here is his card. Call him!"

We waited restlessly until he picked up.

"Samuel here. Who is this?"

"Hi! This is me, Hannah"

"Oh! Hi Hannah! What's up?"

"We found a number and password written in the bind of his diary. The bind was glued tight. There is something that looks like an address too. It can be a locker or something like that. Can you find it?"

"Really? That is a great piece of information! I will look into it. Just mail me the picture!"

"Don't you use WhatsApp?"

"Nah! Not a fan. Mail me."

"Okay, bye."

"Bye"

After mailing him the picture, I felt my appetite returning. I had the feeling that this was not a blind chase.

"Cece, can you buy me something to eat?"

"Only if we watch a movie tonight!"

"Fine!"

Cece jumped up in excitement and we went to the canteen. Since the class was still going on, the canteen was practically empty. There was a boy sitting at a corner table, munching on something and crouching down, looking at his mobile. Cece went ahead and bought two sandwiches. The boy had cleared the table while we got our food, so we sat in the same corner table he was sitting. Cece had this weird habit of stretching her legs out whenever she sat at the table. To avoid being kicked by her, I kept my legs under the chair. That is when something struck my feet.

"What is this?"

"What?"

"There is something under the chair?"

I picked it up. It was a book. There were pictures of angels in the front.

"Is that a hymn book?"

"I don't think so!"

I opened it and my jaw dropped at what I saw.

'The daily register of THE TROUBLED TEENS'

"What? What happened?"

"This is the daily register of the chatroom Joy was in!"

"What the -?"

Just as we were speaking, the boy returned panic stricken. He had certainly come back for the book. When he saw me holding the diary, he ran. I jumped out of my seat and followed him with Cece behind me.

"I must get him. He might have some answers", I thought as I struggled to keep up with him.

CHAPTER EIGHT

The boy was pretty fast. I mean, if it hadn't been for the cleaning lady, I would have never caught him. Before he could run away again, we caught him by his collar and pulled him out of the pile of detergents and mops.

"LEAVE ME!"

"Why did you run?"

"I have class now. I am late!"

"But you came back for something right? Don't you need it?", I said, holding out the diary.

"That is not mine!"

"See, if you are not going to help us, we are going to report to the police that you know something about Joy's death. You know what happens next right? The people who killed Joy would make you disappear the exact same way."

I saw the color draining from his face. Cece signaled to me to go on.

"Look, we want to find the truth as much as you do. But if you are not going to help, Joy's death will be in vain. I know that you don't want that."

"I will talk."

We let go of his collar and he was slowly collecting himself. His face was still pale and he was shaking with fear.

"Can we go somewhere private?"

"Yes!"

We took him to the social service club. The large poster of Joy was still on the wall. Every time I see him, my heart aches. I long for him so much but when I realize he is never going to come back, I lose my sanity. No matter how many times I scream or cry, Joy is gone and I sometimes find it hard to accept that. He went without even leaving memories. All I have of him is the old crimson diary and the love he left behind. Cece saw me zoning out staring at Joy's picture.

"Hannah!"

"Oh! Sorry. What is your name?"

"My name is Chris"

"Did you know Joy personally?"

"No. Joy was the only one who shared his personal details in the chatroom. He never forces anyone to disclose themselves. I knew Joy was in my college but he never knew about me. I was in charge of writing the daily logs. I write them and then scan and send them in the chatroom."

"Did Joy ever discuss about his last mission?"

"Partly yes. I think it was March. Joy told that he might get a new case to work on. During that time, we were discussing corrupt politicians and how we can protest staying within our limits. You know, since most of the members were students, we all wanted to play safe."

"Understandable", said Cece.

"Joy said that this new news might be a big catch and for safety reasons he doesn't want anyone else to get involved unless it is absolutely necessary."

"So, you are telling none of you guys knew about the people who murdered Joy?"

"We had a vague idea. The people Joy was after were very powerful. Not politicians kind of powerful. But the kind that can rule over the ruling people. You get the idea, right?"

"Yes."

He took the diary from my hand and opened it to a page dated 15th August.

"See,

- doing things, no sensible human would do

- not asking for the member's involvement

- Joy will fight them

- Joy said he will find a way

This was the most he said about those people. He made sure not to tell any details so we won't be in trouble. A week before he died, he said that there is a possibility his cover might be broken and if anything happens to him, he asked to delete the chat room immediately."

"So, Joy knew how dangerous it was?"

"Yes"

"Then why did he go for it! He should have asked for help!", I cried loudly.

"He knew the cops couldn't help. That is why he insisted on doing things himself."

I broke down in tears. *"Why did he have to be this reckless? He should have asked for help! He should have talked!"*

Cece thanked Chris and asked him to destroy the diary as soon as possible. She then hugged my crying figure and calmed me down.

"Cece! I would have been there for him. I would have helped him. He should have just talked to me! I wouldn't have let him be alone!"

"Hannah, do you think he would let you into all of this? Even if you were together, he would have kept you away from all this. You know that."

"I couldn't even say goodbye!!!"

Cece couldn't say anything. She hugged me tighter and let me cry it all out.

"How am I supposed to live with this?" I thought as I cried into Cece's arms.

After crying my eyes out, we left the club building and went back into the college. The classes were over and everyone was rushing home.

Cece insisted she dropped me home but I wanted to walk alone. I slowly walked back home drowning in my thoughts. Suddenly Jia came into my mind. I had promised her I would call but I had forgotten it in between all this mess. I dialed Joy's home telephone as soon as I got home.

"Hi! Good evening. Is Jia there?"

"This is Jia's mother. May I know who this is?"

"Hi aunty, I am Hannah, Joy's friend. I just wanted to check on Jia"

"Oh! That is really sweet of you. Wait, I will give the phone to Jia"

I could hear aunty calling Jia. The sadness was still present in her voice.

"Hello, is this Hannah?"

"Yes! I am sorry Jia that I took so long to call you. I was busy"

"It is okay. I am happy you called!"

"How are you?"

"I am okay. I still miss Joy"

"I miss him too. But you know, Joy is watching us from somewhere far away and if he sees us sad because of him he will be sad too. So, let's try to be happy and even when we miss him, let's try thinking of all the happy memories he left us with."

Even as I said this, my eyes welled up and I was trying hard not to let her hear me cry.

"Mm, yes. I will try that"

"Good girl. Note down my number and call me whenever you want to talk, okay?"

"Yes!"

"Okay then baby, I will call you later!"

"Okay bye!"

"By-"

"Wait!", Jia cut me off as I was going to cut the call.

"What happened?"

"Since the last two days, two people have always been standing by the tree opposite our house. They look like bad people."

My heart skipped a beat. I was shaking with fear.

"Will they harm the rest of his family? Or are they there just to check?" A million thoughts ran through my mind.

"It's okay Jia! Don't be scared. I will look into it. For the time being, don't tell anybody about this. Okay?"

"Yes!"

"Okay then, bye! Call me if anything happens, okay?"

"Yes! Bye"

I was freaking out. I cannot let anything bad happen to that family again. The police won't be of any help. So, I decided to call Samuel.

"Hello Samuel"

"Hi Hannah, what's up?"

"Joy's sister said that there are two people standing guard opposite their house. Can you do something about it?"

"Oh my god! Let me see. Did you ask her to not call the police?"

"Yes! Joy's sister is the only one who noticed them until now. I asked her not to say anything to anybody."

"Okay. I will do something about it. We will have to be discrete or else they will find out that we noticed. If that happens things can escalate pretty quickly."

"Yes!"

"Okay! Don't worry. I will sort it out."

"Thanks. Do you have any leads?"

"None. I am still working on it"

"Okay then, bye!"

"Bye!"

I calmed down a little after talking to Samuel. So far, there was nothing solid to work on. We were still on a blank sheet. That boy wasn't much of a help. If only we found the address Joy wrote down, we would have something!

"Please help me with this Joy!"

I prayed silently, desperate for a clue.

CHAPTER NINE

After many days, I was able to get some sleep that night. I think it was 2 AM when my phone rang. I opened my eyes hesitantly, not wanting to give up on the precious sleep I got. When the phone wouldn't stop ringing, I finally got up and took my phone from the bed stand.

"Samuel calling"

"Why is he calling this late?"

As I picked up the call, I already knew that I was not going to hear good news from the other side.

"HELLO!"

"What happened Samuel? Why are you screaming?"

"Chris!"

"What happened to him?"

"HE IS DEAD!"

"WHAT??!!"

"Yes! I just got the information from the police station. His dismembered body was found on the railway tracks!"

"Are you sure it's Chris?! I just talked to him today!"

"It's him. The police are saying this is suicide. I don't think so!"

"Neither do I! He was a member of the chatroom! This isn't a coincidence! Somebody might have found out about him!"

"If they found out about him, we are not safe either."

"What do you mean?", I was sweating. I couldn't process all this information that was coming my way.

"See, you told me you, your friend and me are the only ones who knew about him. That too just hours before. So, if word traveled this fast, none of us are safe. The enemy is close behind us!"

I was shaking. I dragged Cece into this too. What if something happens to her? I wouldn't be able to forgive myself.

"Samuel, are you saying we all are in danger?"

"Yes! You need to get out of your house. Call your friend also. I will pick you up. Send me the address"

"Okay"

"Can I trust him?" At this point, I found it hard to understand who is real and who is not. But right now, Samuel is the only option.

"Cece! I have to call her!"

I dialed Cece's number and waited. She was not picking up.

"Where the hell is this girl?! Why does she sleep so much?"

Cece was not picking up. I texted Samuel that we will pick up Cece on the way and I hurriedly packed a few clothes into my backpack. I left a note on the kitchen counter that I am going trekking with Cece and will be back in a few days. I was pacing up and down my lawn when Samuel's car came to a stop in front of my house.

"Get in! Fast!"

"Samuel what is happening?"

"If I had any clue, we wouldn't be running away to hide at 3 AM!"

"Where are we going?"

"Blue Block"

"That place is dangerous! The entire locality is known for the gangs that operate from there!"

"Trust me it is safer than our house right now! You don't want your family to be in trouble do you? Now tell me where Cece's house is!"

The next twenty or thirty minutes, the only conversation we had was about directions. Samuel was too focused on the road and I was too scared.

"There! That is the house!"

"I will stay in the car. Get her and come fast!"

"Okay!"

I got out of the car and ran to the porch. As I was about to ring the doorbell, I noticed the lock hanging from the handle.

"What the hell! Please God! Don't let this be what I think it is!"

I ran back to the car to get Samuel.

"Samuel!"

"What? Where is she?"

"The door! The door looks like it has been broken into!"

"What the fuck? What the hell are you saying?"

I started crying.

"The door-it is-", I couldn't complete my sentence.

"Fuck it! Come!"

We ran towards the house again. Samuel walked in front of me. We slightly pushed the door open. Samuel turned the flashlight on his phone on.

"Stay behind me"

"Yes"

The hall looked okay. There were no overturned tables and broken vases like I imagined.

"Don't let your guard down!"

We slowly climbed the stairs. The first room to the left is Cece's parents. It was open. Samuel signaled me to follow him there.

The sight that awaited us there was horrifying. Cece's parents were lying face down on their bed with blood splattered everywhere.

"Don't get in! You don't want your fingerprints to be all over here!"

I was too stunned to understand about fingerprints. I was shocked. I couldn't even scream. My body froze.

"Hannah! Wake up! It is not the time to lose your shit! Find Cece!"

Samuel pulled me out of the room but I couldn't still process what I saw. The bodies I saw just a second ago were the warm-hearted people who cooked hot meals for me whenever I came to their house. They were the people who gave me gifts on Christmas, since the day I became friends with Cece. They were my family. And now, they are dead.

"Hannah!" Samuel was shaking and screaming at my face.

"Ye-yes"

"Is this Cece's room?"

"Ye-"

"Okay"

Samuel rushed and opened the door. I expected another blood splattered bedroom but there was nothing. Just an overturned mattress.

"CECE!", I screamed.

"Shut up! Don't scream and wake up people! I think Cece is gone!"

"What do you mean she is gone?", I screamed in between my tears.

"The people who killed Joy, Chris and her parents, they took her!", Sam said with bloodshot eyes.

"What do you mean they took her?!"

"A warning. They might have found out we were looking for them. Someone might have seen us talking or something. If we don't find who the hell these people are, we are going to lose Cece!"

"How can you say that so easily?"

"THIS IS NOT EASY FOR ME! Do you understand?! I HAVE CAUSED THE DEATH OF THREE PEOPLE! Do you think I am happy about that?!"

I just stared at his face. I was at a loss for words.

"If we don't move quickly, things are going to go south! Now come!"

Samuel dragged me out of the house and pushed me into the car. He took off at full speed to Blue Block. The rest of the journey was sad. I was crying loud inside my mind and Samuel was trying hard to stay sane. Suddenly my phone buzzed.

"New text message:

Tell us where Joy kept the evidence and your friend will be safe"

"Samuel!"

"What?"

"They texted", I showed him the text.

"It is like I thought. Someone tipped them off. If my guess is right, it is someone from your college"

"My college?"

"Yes! Someone might have seen you reading Joy's diary. We need to find the evidence as soon as possible or else more lives will be at stake. They don't have a fucking conscience!", Samuel said angrily as he hit the steering wheel.

Anger boiled inside me. First Joy, then Chris and now Cece and her family. I am not going to let them do this again. Now this fight is not just for Joy, it is for me.

"I am not going to let you bastards win!", I cried aloud as Samuel drove past the bright blue sign "**BLUEBLOCK**"

CHAPTER TEN

The car came to a stop in front of a hardware store. The entire neighborhood was shady, but this particular building was the worst! All the courage I mustered up during my journey seemed to drain out of me.

"Get out!"

"Why are we here?"

"This is the hideout I told you about"

"This place? Isn't there somewhere else we can go?"

"Okay. Now listen kid! This is the ONLY option we have. You don't have much of a choice right now. Get out!"

There was no point in arguing. This or death. There was no other option.

The hardware store had a half-broken glass panel in the place of the door. An old bulb was shining in the middle of the store which casted long shadows on the dusty walls.

"George? George, are you there?"

"Who is George?"

"My friend. This is his shop"

A tall skinny man came from somewhere behind the shelves. His denim jacket was worn out and his hairline was slowly receding. His toenails were black with dirt and he was dragging along a pair of really old slippers.

"Hey mate! Why are you here at this hour? Who is this girl?"

"She is my assistant and we are on a mission. We need to stay here for a few days"

"Sure! Climb the stairs at the back of the shelf and close the trapdoor after you. I will bring the food and call you"

"Thank you so much George!"

"No problem"

I think the stairs were the worst maintained part of the store. I took each step in the fear that everything might fall apart. But the room was decent. There was a large bed, a sofa and a cupboard.

"You will have to go down for using the bathroom"

"Oh! Okay"

"Fine. Now let's get to business. Any new messages?"

"None so far. How are we going to find the evidence?"

"No idea"

"What do you mean by that?! My best friend is in danger! My family can be next. Can you please think of something!!"

"See, I understand that you are under pressure, but swearing and screaming at me isn't going to help. Think of what might be the evidence"

I took a few deep breaths and pulled myself together.

"It is not his diary. I read through it. There was nothing in that"

"What can it be then?"

We paced around the room working our brains hard.

"THE ADDRESS", I screamed with all my might.

"What?"

"The one behind Joy's diary! Don't you remember it?"

"Oh yes! But I looked around all the locker rooms coinciding with the area he said. But there was nothing"

"What if it is not a locker?"

"What?"

"What if it is some other place?"

"You mean like a random place? I don't think Joy would be that dumb."

"No! There might be something. He might have left something!"

"What do you think it is?

"The diary! Let me read through it again, I might get something from it!"

Under the flickering yellow bulb, I sat reading the diary while Samuel was fixing up the radio to hear news.

"You need to switch off your phone"

"What? What if my mom calls?"

"They can track us easily with our phones. So, it is for the safety of you and your family"

"Okay" , I said looking down. We were in a maze and the only way was finding the clue.

It was almost daybreak. I was reading through the diary for the third time.

"Please Joy! Help me with this!"

"August 9 2021

I went to the hospital to see Mariam. She has the same blank expression. Nothing changed. The only good thing about this stuffy hospital room is the fountain which can be seen from the window. The view is the best part here. Everything else creeps me out. I hope she can get out of here soon. Staying here might worsen her mind."

"Who the hell is Mariam?"

"What?"

"There is a girl he wrote about. Apparently, she is in some hospital with a great view"

"Hospital with view?"

"Yeah. He can see fountains it seems"

"FOUNTAINS!"

"Woah! Don't scream! What about fountains?"

"Are you really that dumb?! The address Joy wrote! The fountain!"

"What the- why didn't I think about it before?!"

"Maybe you should have been less jealous!"

"Shut up!", my cheeks were going red.

"This is definitely not the time to blush. Get my diary from the bag over there. I have written down about the fountains I saw when I went searching"

"Okay"

We skimmed through the notes Samuel wrote.

"Department store, hotel, spa, HERE! Look, hospital!"

"Yes! This is it!"

"Finally! Joy, you are going to get justice soon"

Suddenly my phone lightened up again.

"New message:

You have 24 hours"

"Shit Samuel! It's them again!"

"Shit! We just have 24 hours to find the evidence and bring them down!"

"What's your plan?"

"We are going to find the evidence and lure them out. We might be needing backup"

"But we can't trust the police, right?"

"No, we can't trust the local police. I have the ultimate card. We have to use it now"

"What is that?"

"National Crime Agency-NCA. The local police might be able to subdue the case but since these people are big shots, they will definitely take an interest."

"Can you trust them?"

"Yes"

"Okay then, let's get going!"

"Yes! This is the final lap!"

CHAPTER ELEVEN

The drive was exhausting. It was partly due to the tension and partly due to the very bad condition of the car. But at this point I don't think I can afford luxury. I wished that I knew how to drive because Samuel looked like he needed help. But all I could ride was a bicycle.

"Are we near?"

"No! There is still a long way to go."

"Do you want to take a rest?"

"Do you want to get killed?"

Okay. That was the end of that conversation. I was feeling unusually calm. Maybe my mind already knew the tension that was going to come hence the calm before the storm. I dozed off sometime later and woke up when the car came to a halt.

"Wake up. We reached"

The hospital looked grand. There were big glass windows and doors and the outside looked more like a hotel than a hospital.

"Are you sure this is the place?"

"Yes"

"But it doesn't look like a normal hospital"

"Because it is not."

"What?"

"This is a mental hospital"

"What??!"

"Are you deaf?"

"Sorry"

"Come on! We don't have time. What did you say the kid's name was?"

"Mariam"

"Okay come on!"

Two well-dressed security guards stood by the door and greeted us politely. Samuel kept on turning back.

"Why are you looking behind?"

"To see if someone is following us"

"Do you think they tailed us?"

"There is a possibility for everything now"

The receptionist greeted us with an even wider smile.

"Why is everyone so happy here?"

"If you are wondering why everyone is happy here, it is to boost the morale of patients and bystanders"

"Did you just read my mind?"

"It is evident on your face"

"Oh! Sorry"

"Hi ma'am. Good morning"

"Good morning! How can I help you?"

"We are here to see a patient named Mariam"

"Oh! Let me see. Yes sure, you can meet her. Can I know your name?"

"John"

"And this lady here?"

"She is my daughter. Amanda"

I tried hard not to show the varying facial expressions.

"Thank you. Room 198. The lift is to your right"

"Thank you!"

We walked towards the lift with golden panels.

"Oh! So the number was the room number. Are you sure they won't rat us out?"

"Yes, or else the evidence would have already been in the other people's hand"

"Yeah"

"Did you get any new messages?"

"No. They already gave us a deadline, remember?"

"Yes. Hurry"

Room 198 was the saddest place I had ever been to. The curtains were drawn and empty picture frames hung on the wall. On the old bedding, a frail figure was lying covered up in thick blankets. As I moved closer to her, I saw the emptiness in her eyes. I think since Joy is not here, her condition might have deteriorated.

"She looks as if she has only days left"

"Yes"

My eyes were fixed on the figure on the bed. She was not even moving.

"Where do you think the evidence is?"

"What?"

"This is not the time to sympathize! Your friend's, family's and our lives depend on this. Fast!"

"Yes"

I pulled myself together and rummaged through the cupboards and drawers. We found nothing more than dull clothes and old bedsheets.

"I don't think there is anything here"

"There should be or else we are dead!"

"Who are you?"

A lady in her early thirties was standing at the door. She looked furious. We froze at our respective positions and stared at her.

"Who the hell are you?"

"Hi"

"I asked who you are, mister?"

"Hi I am Samuel, I am a journalist and this is Hannah."

"Why are you searching this room?"

We didn't respond and just looked at each other.

"Answer me or I will call the police!"

"Relax! She is Joy's friend"

"Joy?"

"Yes! I am Joy's friend. He had mentioned in his diary about this place. There is a clue here and we need to find it. There are too many lives at stake"

"Wait here!"

The lady walked out quickly. We stood frozen in our spots and looked at each other in doubt.

"Will she call the police?"

"I don't think so"

The lady came back again and closed the door quickly.

"This is what you are looking for", she said, showing a red pen drive.

"What is this?"

"This is the evidence Joy left before he died"

"Do you have a laptop? We need to see this", asked Samuel.

"There is one in the bottom drawer"

While Samuel was starting the laptop, the lady came near me and smiled. "You look just like he talked about"

My eyes started filling up.

"Did he talk a lot about me?"

"Yes", she said with a sad smile. "You guys would have looked great together"

I couldn't hold back my tears anymore. The lady hugged me close and let me cry on her shoulders.

"I wish I had met him before too!", I cried louder.

"Don't cry! Joy wouldn't like this"

"I miss him! I wish at least we talked before he-", I cried louder.

"It's okay. It's okay. Don't cry"

I pulled out of the hug and wiped my tears.

"Who is she?", I asked, looking at Mariam.

"She is Joy's friend and one of the reasons Joy got into all the mess"

"What?", both of us looked at the lady in shock.

"What do you mean she is one of the reasons?"

"Well, that is a long story"

"Well, we are all ears. We need as much information as possible to solve this", said Samuel.

CHAPTER TWELVE

"Mariam was Joy's family friend. Their families were friends long before they were born. Mariam and Joy practically grew up together. Mariam's and Joy's father were journalists. Jacob and Daniel were the best in their field. They ran their own newspaper called "The Real Truth". Just like the name, they aimed to bring forward unfiltered news to the public. And for the very same reason, they had a lot of enemies."

"I remember the newspaper. They were an inspiration for all journalists. I really wanted to meet them but then the paper shut down suddenly one day and there was no news of them", said Samuel.

"Yes. They always made sure not to publicize their personal information because that would put their family in danger. To be honest, even the kids were not aware of their father's job. I met Jacob and Daniel almost two years ago. I was working in a public mental health center. That hospital was a mess. As a nurse, I did all I could to alert the authorities about the bad condition of the hospital but nothing changed. I knew that they were hiding things from the staff. Jacob called me one evening and asked if I can cooperate with them to bring out the injustice done to the patients. They promised to protect me if I gave them intel. I was asked to keep a close eye on the superintendent after work hours. So, one day I stayed back after my shift was over. I was going through the inventory of the pharmacy and found medicines that we did not need in the hospital. I took the picture of the inventory list and sent it to Jacob."

"Did the superintendent sell medicines for extra profit?"

"That would have been far better than what we actually found out"

Her eyes were slowly getting teary.

"Jacob told me the next day that these medicines were actually used during organ transplants and some of them are said to cause brain death. I was shocked. I had no idea why we needed these medicines. I stayed back consecutively for the next few days. One evening I saw a male nurse taking a patient out of the ward. I was not familiar with his face. I asked him where he was taking the patient and he calmly replied that he was taking the patient for shock treatment. I stood there puzzled wondering because he was taking a perfectly calm patient for shock treatment.

I followed him and decided to take a look at what was happening inside. What I saw through the small creek of the window was shocking. The perfectly healthy patient was given some injections and after a few minutes they cut him open and took out all the healthy organs. I had the presence of mind to record whatever was happening even though I was in shock. I ran to the superintendent's room to report this and before pushing open the door I heard muffled cries from inside. I went around the office room and through the ventilation window I saw the superintendent molesting a patient. I was stunned. I filmed the superintendent and ran out of the hospital before anyone saw me. I mailed the details to Jacob. He was horrified and promised me that he would bring this to the public's attention. The headline of their newspaper the next day was about the hospital. I left the city that day itself because I was scared of my safety. Even though the probability of me getting caught was low, I didn't want to risk it. I mailed them a resignation letter before I left."

"I remember the news. It caused quite a ruckus. The entire government was shaking. The ministers were running left and right"

"Yes. It caused a huge commotion"

I felt quite dumb because it was my first-time hearing about the incident. The horrifying details of the incident created a huge pain in my chest. I wondered if there were such people in this world.

"Jacob didn't contact me after the news went public. The news stated that a wealthy co-operation was behind all this and the said corporation has a very good reputation among the public. I felt scared for both of them because now matters were getting serious. All the other newspapers slowly forgot about this incident but Jacob's newspaper always had a column reserved for this. They didn't let go of this. After five or six months, I got a call while I was working. I was working as a home nurse then. It was Joy."

"Joy?"

"Yes. He was crying when I picked up the phone. He said that he was Daniel's son and needed my help immediately. The name caught my attention quickly and I asked him to calm down. He told me how Mariam's parents were tortured and murdered right before her eyes and how they caused an accident to kill Joy's entire family. I was shocked. I couldn't believe this was happening. I never thought Jacob and Daniel would be caught. Joy asked my help to admit Mariam to a good mental hospital and to personally take care of her. Apparently, Daniel had left my name and contact number in his diary which was hidden in his safe.

Joy was angry and sad. He wanted to get revenge on the people who did this to Mariam's and his family. I promised him that I will take care of Mariam and asked him not to get revenge as they are very dangerous people. Joy was not ready to listen. He said that it was his duty not just to their parents but also to the people. I moved with Mariam to this hospital. No one came for us all this while. This was why I was rude when I first saw you."

"It's understandable."

"A week before Joy died, he came here late at night. He handed me over this pen drive and asked me to hide it. He looked tired and scared. I asked him what happened but he did not say anything. I pleaded with him to stop whatever he was after but he said that it is almost the end and if he gave up now all his efforts would be in vain. The next thing I hear is that Joy is dead. I knew what happened to him but I was helpless. I wanted to shout out to the world that it was a murder but I was scared. I also had the responsibility of looking after Mariam. I couldn't act recklessly. I am sorry"

"You don't have to be sorry. You did what we all would do if we were in your shoes. We will bring all this into light"

"Thank you so much!", she said and cried into her hands. I understood how suffocating she might have felt.

Samuel plugged the pen drive into the laptop. It contained a password protected folder. He typed in my birthday as the password which was mentioned in Joy's diary as well beneath the room number. The folder opened. It contained the evidence his dad collected then about the hospital and also new evidence that Joy had collected. The organ and human trafficking were happening in a number of mental hospitals around the country. We were shocked beyond words. The next folder in the pen drive was what shocked us the most. The culprit. The culprit was none other than the chairman of 'G King holdings' the biggest real estate owner in the country. All the news about him being a generous and kind man and how he built his company through hard work was all a lie.

He fooled everyone for years. I stood frozen. There was a group picture among the pictures Joy took. It looked like the inauguration ceremony of some sort of charity event and I recognized a face standing next to the chairman.

"I remember that face from somewhere!"

"Who?"

"The one standing next to the chairman"

"You mean this blue suit?"

"Yes. Wait! Found it!"

"Who is he?"

"He is the principal's secretary!"

"What?"

"He is the secretary of my college principal!"

"What the -!! Now we know how they found us!"

"Shit! That bastard! He is the reason they took my Cece!"

I was flaming with anger.

"Don't lose your cool!"

"How can I not?!!", I glared at Samuel.

"We need to find this rat before he finds us. First, we need to hand over the evidence. Remember, Cece is still with them and we don't have time."

"ARGH! FINE! What should we do now?"

"Hand over evidence first. Come let's get out of here. We will call the NCA on our way. Staying here might be dangerous for Mariam."

"Yes"

"Thank you so much sister for helping us. We will take care of things"

"Thank you", she said, sobbing.

Before we got out, I looked at Mariam's fragile body once more.

"Joy, I will bring justice to your efforts. Your death won't be in vain!"

"That bloody bastard Richard!", Samuel said while getting on the lift.

"Richard?"

"That is the chairman's name. Richard Cottingham"

"Woah. Hey! You said no phones! Whose phone is that?", I said pointing to the old Nokia handset in Samuel's hand.

"Don't scream! This is Plan B. You get into the car. I will come."

"Why do we need a plan B now?"

"Just wait by the car. I will come"

I waited for like five minutes near the car. I saw Samuel running towards the car smiling. "What the hell is he smiling for?"

Suddenly a big black car hit Samuel. His body flew up and hit a lamppost by the road. One second, I saw Samuel smiling and the next thing I saw was his lifeless body hitting the road. Blood was oozing steadily from his head. I stood frozen in shock for a second. Then I ran towards him screaming. Suddenly a tall man with a huge body stopped me in my tracks. I looked at him bewildered and tried to push past him to get to Samuel. He stopped me and pulled me by my collar and said, "Found you!"

CHAPTER THIRTEEN

I don't remember when I lost my consciousness. But when I came to, my hands and legs were tied with something really strong. I was lying down on the floor and I could feel the floor being wet. Coldness was seeping through my body. My eyes were shut tight and the darkness started to scare me. I tried to sit up but my efforts were in vain. I screamed and shouted for help. As my cries got louder, I heard footsteps coming towards me. Someone lifted me up from the floor and took off my blindfold. It took me a while to adjust to the surroundings. The room was really smaller than what I had pictured it to be. The walls were covered in moss with paint falling off. The only source of light was from a small creek on the roof. The man who came inside was very tall and well built. He was wearing a big blue hoodie and jeans. He smiled widely at me as I was struggling to keep my eyes open. His unkempt hair and stained teeth scared me much more than the cold floor and darkness.

"Is my doll up?"

"Who the hell are you people?! Where is Sam?"

"You are prettier in person. I now understand why your boyfriend was all concerned about you!"

"Boyfriend? What the hell are you talking about? Where is Sam?"

"You really won't shut up, will you?"

"Who the hell are you to ask me to shut up?! You creep!"

A tight slap landed on my face. I fell down. Those big arms pulled me up and cut the zip tie on my feet. He then dragged me out. We were walking along a narrow corridor. I tried my best to wriggle out his grip but he was too strong. He pushed me into a room that looked like the living room of a house. Few men were sitting on an old sofa and watching football game on the small tv propped up on the wall. All of them looked equally scary as the one who was pushing me into the room. The stench of alcohol and weed filled the room.

"WHO THE HELL ARE YOU PEOPLE AND WHY AM I HERE?"

"Too many questions, doll! We have prepared a small surprise for you!", said one of the men who was chugging down alcohol from a bottle. He was double the size of the one who brought me and scarier. I felt cold shivers going down my spine. I tried my best to not show it on my face.

"Where the hell is Sam?"

The man who was standing next to me pushed me to a window. He then signaled someone standing on the other side to open it. What I saw was horrifying. Cece was tied to a chair. Her face was drooping down and blood was dripping from her head.

"CECE! CECE! WAKE UP!!!!! CECE IT IS ME HANNAH! CECE!"

She tried to lift her head to look at me but she couldn't. I couldn't bear the sight I was seeing. Anger boiled up inside me.

"WHAT THE HELL DID YOU DO TO HER YOU MONSTERS? ARE YOU ANIMALS?? YOU BASTARDS!"

I kicked the chair next to me and screamed and shouted at them. The man who ordered them to open the window came up to me and slapped me again. This hurt much more than before but the anger piling up inside me neutralized the physical pain. I glared at him and got up. He was coming closer to slap me again.

"Don't you dare touch me you monster!"

He let out a shrill laugh. The entire room went silent. Somebody had turned off the television. "Now I know why all those men walked right into their death for you?"

"What do you mean?"

"You still don't know, do you? That over smart reporter who helped you, he is lying frozen in a mortuary now. Also, your boyfriend! You know what happened to him right?"

"My boyfriend? Who are you talking about?"

"Joy! That dumb boy. He thought that all that confidence in a chat room could actually help him in the real world. He didn't come to meet us even when we threatened to harm his family but then we found his weakness!! When we showed him your beautiful pictures, he voluntarily walked right into his death! That fool!"

"What are they saying? No! No! It can't be! Joy didn't die because of me! It can't be!" I was losing my head. I couldn't believe that Joy died because of me.

"Did you love me that much to actually walk into death for me? Why didn't you tell me? We could have found a way! Why did you do all this alone?"

"NO!!!!!!!"

"Is my doll losing her mind? Hahaha!! This is a fun sight to watch!"

"No! Joy didn't die for me! No! It can't be!", I couldn't take it anymore. I fell down and cried. All the drive for revenge seemed to seep out of me. I didn't want to believe that Joy died for me. I didn't want to believe that his love for me was so much that he gave up his revenge and life for me. He even jeopardized his family's safety for me. All those thoughts were making me weak from inside. Joy, Cece's parents, Sam they all died for me. I couldn't take it anymore. A part of me knew that dying in these monster's hands was not what they all wanted for me. But right now, I couldn't find a way out. Everything was weighing me down.

"You shouldn't give up now Hannah! Get yourself together! Find a way out of this mess"

Yes! I have to rescue Cece! Even if my life is of no value now, I couldn't let them kill Cece. I already have enough blood on my hands. I got up on my feet.

"Okay doll, we will give you a chance to save your pretty friend back there. Why don't you tell us where you hid the evidence? It wasn't in your car or on the reporter's body, so now tell me. You don't want more blood on your hands do you?"

"I have it on me. It is hidden under my dress."

One of them approached me.

"Stop right there! Untie me. I won't let any of you touch me. I have nothing more to lose. I will give you the pen-drive. Just untie me."

"YOU FOOL!", one of them screamed.

"Shh! She can't run away, can she? Just untie her."

"Boss-"

"Just do as you are told"

One of them approached me and started to cut the zip tie on my arms. Just as he finished cutting my zip tie, I turned around and grabbed the knife from him and stabbed him in the thighs. I then dashed towards the man they called boss. There was total commotion and before I could reach him, I heard a loud bang and I fell face down on the floor. The last thing I remember seeing was my own blood puddling near my face from my chest.

"Joy, will this be the end?", I thought before I closed my eyes.

CHAPTER FOURTEEN

Lights flickered on and out. I was being dragged, lifted, placed onto something and pushed around. I was trying to call out for help but my voice kept getting stuck inside me. I felt myself drift out of me. My eyes were fighting to be kept open. Some part of me knew that if I shut my eyes, I might lose myself forever.

Suddenly a familiar face drifted in front of my eyes. The same silver eyes I fell for. He was bending over me, telling me something. I tried to lift my head to hear better.

"Hannah..."

"Joy!", even though all my senses were slowly shutting down, I could recognize him. His silver orbs and hazelnut hair. I struggled to keep my eyes open so I could keep on seeing his face. His cold hands touched my cheek gently. Tears were coming down his eyes.

"You should live. This is not what I wanted for you"

"Joy, I shall come with you"

"No. You need to stay here. Please"

Suddenly his figure started getting blurred. His cold hands were slowly retreating from my cheeks.

"Joy...Joy!"

He disappeared right before my eyes. I kept on calling him. I kept on reaching out to him. But he wasn't there. He is gone. It became harder to breathe. I felt like I was being drowned in something really dense. I wanted to shout out to save me but my voice kept on getting stuck inside me. I could hear people shouting my name but I couldn't see them.

"Driver! Hurry up! We are losing the patient! Hannah! Stay with us! Hannah!"

"I need to live, I cannot die like this."

When I opened my eyes, I saw my mom's worry-stricken face looking down at me.

"Mom"

"Hannah! Love, are you awake?"

"Where is Cece?"

"She is fine. She is resting in the room next to ours. Don't worry. How are you feeling?"

"I am ok, I guess."

"Take a rest. The doctor asked you to take a lot of rest! We were worried sick about you!"

"Where is Dad?"

"He is with Cece"

"What happened? I thought they killed me!"

"Before leaving the hospital, Sam sensed something wrong and hid the pen-drive in the hospital washroom. He then informed the NCA about the evidence and left the hospital. Just like his suspicions, they came at you guys in front of the hospital."

"What the-? So did the NCA get the evidence?"

"Yes."

"Thank God! But how did they find me?"

"Sam hid a GPS tracker inside your pocket. They tracked your location and rescued Cece and you. If they had been even a minute late, we would have lost both of you."

"Sam you! You really did a good job! Why did you have to die?" I thought. A small smile came to my face. Even though we knew each other for a short time, Sam had become

someone really important to me. If it had not been for him, Joy wouldn't have received the justice he deserved. He is someone I will be thankful for until I die.

"So is Joy's case closed?"

"Yes, the chairman and all his men were caught and arraigned. The chairman received life imprisonment. G King holdings is shut down. All the shareholders have withdrawn and the company will be sold at a very cheap price to someone. Also, the doctors who cooperated with them were also caught."

"Finally, it has come to an end."

"Yes. Now, you have to take care of yourself! Okay?"

"Yes Mom", I replied with a smile.

"Joy, we did it! All your efforts weren't in vain. We brought the truth to light."

Finally, things settled down. The number of people who lost their lives due to this were so many. A part of me will always be guilty that I couldn't save them. A part of me will always regret that I could not be there for Joy when he needed me the most. I could have stopped a lot of things from happening. I couldn't. But at least now, I made sure that they won't happen again.

While I was drowning in my thoughts, a tall man appeared by the door.

"Excuse me, may I come in?"

My mom got up looking worried and scared. I became alert too.

"Don't worry, I am Lee Jong In. I work with the NCA.", he flashed an I.D card. My mom let out a sigh.

"I am sorry. We were just worried. Please come in"

"I can understand. How are you doing Hannah?"

"Better", I said, smiling a bit.

"I came here because there is something you need to see."

He then sat down on the chair nearby and opened the laptop he was carrying. I looked puzzled at my mom.

"There is a video we retrieved from Joy's phone which we found from the scene where you were rescued. He had left a video message for you. We thought you would want to see this."

My heart started to beat faster. Tears were already struggling to flow out of my eyes. I sat up to have a better look at the laptop. My mom came by my side and slightly squeezed my shoulders.

The detective turned the laptop towards me and pushed the play button.

"Hi Hannah! If you are seeing this, I might have already been dead. How are you doing? I hope you are doing great. This is not how I wanted to talk to you first. I wanted to come see you with flowers and chocolates. I wanted to take you out on nice dates. I wanted us to fight over silly things. I wanted us to be like every other couple out there. And I wanted to watch you walk down the aisle to me. Hah! I thought I had time. I had to sort out a few things. Thought I could come to you after I sorted them. But life isn't fair and hence, this is how we will talk for the first and the last time.

Hannah, I love you. I have loved you since the day I saw you. I remember how you came to college on the first day with sleepy eyes, with your friend dragging you in. Haha! You looked really funny but really cute too! I fell in love right then. Every time I saw you, my heart kept on beating faster and faster. I would wait to see you during the social service club meetings but you rarely made it. I never wasted any moment that I could steal a glance at

you. You are the most beautiful person I have seen. It's funny how I have an entire folder full of your pictures but I never talked to you in person. Jia always used to make fun of me about this. That silly girl doesn't know how difficult it is. Let her fall in love herself, only then will she know!

Anyways, I love you, Hannah. I wish I could have said this to you in person. But yeah, here we are. Even though I am not with you now, I will live on in your heart. I hope you live a happy and long life. If there is a next life, I will not hesitate to come to you. Goodbye Hannah! Take care. I love you."

I broke down in tears. Mom hugged me close.

"I am sorry", said the detective looking guilty.

"It's okay", said Mom, hugging me close.

"I think I will leave now", he said getting up.

"Can you give me that clip?" I asked, sobbing uncontrollably.

"This still needs to be processed. Once the formalities are over, I will hand over the video", he said and left the room.

"Mom! He loved me so much! Why didn't he say anything!! WHY???? Why can't we be together? I need him Mom! He died because of me!"

I couldn't stop crying. The fact that I will never be with Joy was hitting me hard. I couldn't accept that he will never be back. I think a part of me believed that once I uncovered the truth, Joy would magically run into my arms. I couldn't accept this. I couldn't accept the fact that Joy will never be with me.

"Hannah love, it's okay baby! It's not because of you baby, don't cry! Please don't cry baby! Please!", my mom started crying too.

"He deserved better, Mom!"

"Yes, baby he did. He did."

"How am I supposed to live without you Joy? It was easier when I did not know how much you loved me! I love you Joy! I love you! Please come to me!"

CHAPTER FIFTEEN

1 year later

I woke up when the sun hit my sleeping face. I got out of the bed and unwillingly walked to my mirror. The black bags under my eyes are partially gone. I have been sleeping well these days. After the incident, I had to go to a therapist to get over everything that happened. Sleep was a luxury I couldn't afford during the initial months. Even though I did not want to take any medicine, I had to take them eventually because my health was getting worse from my lack of sleep.

I combed my hair and tied it up into a bun. Today is a special day. It has been a year since Joy passed away. I made plans with Jia to visit his grave. Cece is still in physical therapy. So, we thought of visiting her after visiting Joy. My phone rang suddenly, it was Jia.

"Hello! Hannah! Did you wake up?"

"Yes, yes! Are you getting ready?"

"Yes! Mom and grandpa just came back after visiting Joy"

"Really? I will be ready soon. Meet you at the church"

"Okay! Bye"

I kept my phone on the dressing table. A wide smiling Joy was looking at me with his silver eyes. The little framed picture on my dressing table has been giving me strength all these months. His smile is the reason I want to wake up and do well. Even though Joy has left me a year back, he is still living inside me. He is the fire that keeps me going.

The months after the incident, I spent a lot of time learning how Joy was as a person. Apart from the responsible son who fought the injustice against his family, he was a joyful brother, a very goofy friend and a good student. Knowing bits and pieces about him from his family and friends pulled me closer to him. Many times, my mom tried to make me move on but I held on. Nowadays she doesn't pressure me. She knows that he is the reason that keeps me going.

I dressed in a light pink dress. Jia had told me that Joy always liked it when I dressed in light pink. So, I decided to go for it today. I took a taxi to the church. When I got there, Jia was already inside praying. I quietly sat behind her and thanked God for giving me the strength to survive.

"Oh! Hannah! When did you get here?"

"Just a while ago. I didn't want to disturb you"

"Ah! Come, let's go see Joy"

The walk to the graveyard was filled with awkward silence. It was Jia who broke the ice. "How is your therapy going? Are you getting any sleep?"

"Yes, I am getting better"

"How is Cece?"

"She is still at the rehabilitation center. The doctor says she needs a few more months of physical therapy"

"Oh! Where will she stay once she is alright?"

"I am planning to bring her home with me. If she gets better by this year, we will rejoin our classes together next year"

"That's nice! We have reached"

Joy's grave was already filled with a variety of flowers from his friends and family. It feels good to know that so many of them are still remembering him. I kneeled down and lit a candle that I brought with me. We sat silently for a while.

"Oh! You brought his favorite flowers", said Jia.

"Yes", I said with a smile.

Joy's mother had told me that Joy loved daisies the most. They mean innocence and purity. Joy was too good a soul for this world. It's sad that he left early. He deserved better.

"Hannah, until when are you going to hang onto Joy? You know that you need to live a life on your own right?", asked Jia as we were walking back.

"I am not really sure. A part of me knows that I need to move on. I know that I need to forget about Joy. But, I can't. It's not that I wake up and cry every day that I lost him. He gives me a reason to wake up and fight for myself. He is the only reason I did not succumb after all that happened."

"I know"

"Don't worry, I won't go mad. I am strong! You know that right?", I said by flexing my biceps.

"Hehe! Yes"

"Come on, let's go see Cece"

"Yes!"

My life has been divided into two parts. Before Joy and after him. Even though the second part was filled with so much pain, sorrow and difficulties, it also did help me learn a lot about myself. By knowing about Joy, I came to discover a part of me that even I didn't know existed. The journey was tough, but today I am a better person than I have been my entire life. After Cece gets back, we will start going to college. Unlike before, I have a dream now. I dream to be a source of support to all the kids out there who need help. I always had the regret that if Joy had a reliable person to talk to, he wouldn't have died alone. So, instead of drowning in guilt, I decided to do something about it. Therefore, after finishing my studies I plan to open a center for kids and young adults so they have a safe space to come to. As baby steps to my dream, I have already started volunteering in various youth shelters. Speaking to the kids and being a comfort for them makes me feel more at ease. I can proudly say that I am loving my life now.

The journalist association acknowledged Sam's effort to bring the truth and awarded him the highest recognition they have. If Sam would have been alive, he would take the award, down a few pegs and swear at them for only realizing his talent now. I miss his swearing and petty fights sometimes.

Joy left this world giving all of us something beautiful to hold on to. His death and his life was never in vain. I don't know how long I will hold on to him. But until then,

"I love you Joy!"

Printed by Libri Plureos GmbH in Hamburg, Germany